*The
Invention
of Truth*

THE
INVENTION
OF TRUTH

Marta Morazzoni

Translated from the Italian by
M. J. Fitzgerald

Alfred A. Knopf   New York

1993

THIS IS A BORZOI BOOK
PUBLISHED BY ALFRED A. KNOPF, INC.

Copyright © 1993 by Alfred A. Knopf, Inc.

Originally published in Italy as *L'Invenzione della Verita*
by Longanesi & C., Milan, in 1988.

Copyright © 1988 by Longanesi & C.

Library of Congress Cataloging-in-Publication Data
Morazzoni, Marta [date]
[Invenzione della verità. English]
The invention of truth / Marta Morazzoni ; translated from
the Italian by M. J. Fitzgerald.
p. cm.
ISBN 0-394-58088-5
1. Bayeux tapestry—Fiction. 2. Ruskin, John, 1819–1900—
Fiction. 3. Amiens (France)—History—Fiction.
PQ4873.o663I5813 1993
853'.914—dc20   92-25047
CIP

Manufactured in the United States of America
Published May 21, 1993
Second Printing, July 1993

for Piera

The
Invention
of Truth

THEY SAY THAT once upon a time a group of expert needlewomen gathered for a long time in a minor court of France up in the north. There is no record of any official proclamation or of any messengers sent from region to region to encourage the quiet migration of these women. And in fact the migration happened, one could say, by word of mouth, so that no needlewoman of any talent remained ignorant of the appeal, not one escaped or wanted to escape the call.

They left carrying very little, not to be burdened with anything superfluous on the journey: all each one needed was a thimble and a roll of fabric tightly padded with cotton, in which an armory of needles of different sizes rested in disciplined order. For some of the needlewomen the thimble was of silver and the roll was of silk, made precious by embroidered monograms, but for all the container was colored and decorated: unrolled, it showed at the top the thorough array of needles in ascending order of size, from the finest to the thickest, and underneath the long needles for the thicker cloths, which brushed with their eyes the points of the needles above.

The departure of so many embroideresses was solitary, and solitary too was the journey. But none was discouraged by the distance to be traveled, and all reached their destination. It happened that at times, on their way, they recognized one another as directed by the same destiny and for the same reasons. France was a land whose gentle landscape was interspersed by numerous wild forests, through which ran, especially in the north, dark unfrequented paths. But all the women reached the place of assignation without accident. They say there were three hundred.

A young queen with a ringing name waited for them at the court. She was a devoted wife to a husband with whom she was not in love, but for whose life she had feared on a day not long before. She was proud of the way she had succeeded in dominating her fear and her terror of a possible defeat. During the days when the terror gripped her, she had formulated a vow as a sign of her great gratitude if the anguish should be dissolved and she should finally return to reign in a kingdom at peace. It had been

mostly at night, in the expectant silence of sleepless-
ness, that she had sketched a project in her mind: she
thought of a writing comprehensible to everyone, to
which everyone would draw near with excitement
and be moved. She imagined some kind of undefined
universal book, from whose perfection no language
was excluded, to whose tones no ear could be deaf.
She slept only when she thought she had found it,
and in her sleep continued to perfect it. The writing
required a sheet of linen, and the next day she called
her ladies-in-waiting and servants, ordered them to
secure some flax, and for many days she and they
spun and wove until they had made a strong, thin
cloth. They prepared seventy meters of it, white
closely woven material; then the word began to spread
and the needlewomen set out.

THE ROAD THAT SLOPES from the Pas-de-Calais and
runs this side of the coast, just touching the town of
Abbeville, was never heavily used. When a straight
line was drawn to Paris, the whole of Picardy was
left on the edge, joining the forgotten lands and ar-
bitrarily reduced to poverty and neglect. Its capital,
Amiens, fell into silence. In any case, it already was
an ugly city.

It was already ugly when Ruskin saw it; a cloudy
river, the Somme, ran through it, the houses and

streets were opaque in all seasons, and they became ever gloomier during the autumn rains. At least in the good seasons the countryside lent the town its own habitual melancholy and affectionate sweetness, giving it a certain brightness of color, perhaps through the ordered alignment of poplars, or the well-tended fields with their impression of dignified poverty.

At Amiens the streets follow the contour of the hill, in fact nothing more than a low hillock that struggles to dominate the surrounding plain. The town has no memory of the time when it was the capital of the kingdom that was to become France, since France had grown and forgot and abandoned it, as a degenerate daughter might abandon her mother. But perhaps it was precisely for this reason that Amiens aroused Ruskin's interest: this dirty and unflirtatious town had severed all links with its past save one, the unchangeable grandeur of its cathedral.

It cannot be called the most beautiful cathedral in France; it has too many external imperfections, and the stone is overabundant and liable to form crevices as it breaks off. The effect is contradictory, both of majesty and awkwardness. Whoever has seen Chartres in the silence of a moonlit night can perhaps understand what majesty is, and Ruskin must have experienced it on his journeys through France. And yet, by more than any other wonder, he had been attracted to the cumbersome seigneury of Picardy, rocked by the swaying plane trees and the birches along the river. The cathedral continued to attract him, and he made it the destination of his last journey. By then he was already old, and leaving his hermitage on the shore of a lake in Scotland was a great effort. He still shuddered at the memory of the crossing of the channel, with the shiver of excitement of a child and much more: the spires of Abbeville had astounded him, and now he waited for them, for the anticipation of known emotion is an even greater pleasure than the excitement of surprise. Soon after the two spires of Abbeville disappear from sight, the train draws near Amiens, and enters an ugly station from which an even uglier city is visible. One morning in October 1879, Ruskin and a few other passengers alighted from the Calais train; with him was his valet and photographer, George.

THE QUEEN HAD WANTED to proffer a welcome without any discrimination to the needlewomen who had completed the journey. She wanted the old as well as the young to find becoming accommodation, but the court was small and could not receive all the women within the palace walls. There were truly many, though it seemed to the queen there were barely enough to fulfill the writing she had in mind.

By order of her majesty, homes outside the palace walls were opened in hospitality, and the queen provided a sum sufficient to support the women, to which she added a reward for the generosity and the sacrifices undertaken by those ready to welcome the strangers. The arrangements were extraordinarily generous for the times, a sign of how dearly the queen held the project and how determined she was to bring it to completion. Finding a home and a table and directing the movements of each woman was an arduous task. The people of the area watched the women, unsure whether to fear or ignore them: they were certainly a quaint invasion into the world of the village. There were moments of impatience and intolerance, and at times there was the risk that order would degenerate into chaos. But the uncertainty did not last; soon the differences were settled, and were replaced by expectancy and a peaceful alertness.

The cloth had been ready for some time, stored in a room in the palace and covered by a black sheet to prevent it from yellowing in the light and from being soiled by dust. But the work could not begin yet: the queen was not satisfied with the designs submitted by her artisans. The embroidery had to show the actions of noblemen and knights, of horsemen and foot soldiers and common people. The action had to take place against a background of vast plains, hills, and sea. And at the end the vanquished and the

victorious had to fill the bloody battlefield like looming giants, the slaughtered and the triumphant.

Day after day the artists called by the queen
worked and elaborated the complex theme. But she
was never satisfied by their efforts, she wanted something more complete, clearer. Above all she wanted
something nimbler: in her mind the lightness of the
embroidery was the key to the writing.

She would pause for a long time in front of the
sketches, imagining on cloth the slight but penetrating
transcript. Each time she would reject what she saw
with an impatient gesture: it wasn't what she wanted;
and she asked herself anxiously when she would come
across the perfection she sought. The disquiet was
shared by the artists themselves, who doubted that
they understood the queen's wishes. Then, one morning, they found her obstinately bent over a table
sketching the ugly outline of a palace. Under the
arches of the palace a lord was seated on a throne, in
discussion with two subjects: the hand of the queen
was hesitant, and the sketch on the paper was childish,
but the intention was finally clear. To make it even
clearer the clumsy artist had traced with uncertain
script above the palace the name of the lord: Edward.

AMIENS IN 1879 was a charmless and disorderly
industrial town, blackened by smoke from factories.

The Invention of Truth

For the gentleman who had just alighted from the train and was standing on the platform with the minimum luggage of the well-seasoned traveler, this was the first journey after three years of voluntary exile in a forgotten corner of Scotland. It had not been easy to decide to undertake the trip, considering the effort it cost him and the sudden bewilderments that seized him and from which he had difficulty in defending himself. From which in fact he no longer tried to defend himself.

He still looked good, barely heavier than he had been in his youth. His memory, when not victim of the sudden confusions and fluctuations, was excellent. For example, he remembered everything of Amiens, even the irrelevant detail of the statue that at one time had been in the southern portal, of Saint-Honoré, patron saint of pastry cooks. It is merely a curious detail, nevertheless among the suggestions that the scholar would make to visitors of the town, there would be a specific one: not to fail to visit a *boulangerie*, even before making for the cathedral. He had probably been tempted to suggest which *boulangerie* and for what, but had refrained and limited himself to indicating the only possible route from the station to the church, a route that narrowed down the choice of shops to the ones that he himself never failed to visit. It was one way of propitiating the patron saint of such a pleasurable art, whom the town had so unjustly removed from his niche and exiled to the cold, northern portal.

Some travelers who were running to catch the train for Paris had to swerve, muttering, to avoid the gentleman who blocked the way, standing still on the platform as if undecided. He made up his mind only at the whistle of the departing train, and motioned to his companion, who picked up a large package that had been leaning against a bench. Together they walked to the exit: there were some cabs waiting at the front, and the gentleman called one with a peremptory gesture. When it drew up they busied themselves loading the light luggage and the cumbersome package, which they placed carefully on the seat. George had to reach the hotel (the usual one, which Ruskin had used since the journeys in his youth) and examine the room, a task of utmost importance, given the habit of the master to make of every hotel room a sort of last refuge. As for the gentleman, he started down the rue Trois Cailloux, beyond the courthouse. He remembered this street perfectly: a little farther on there was one of those modest bakeries that was nonetheless excellently supplied. England never offers anything quite as simple and fragrant as a croissant mingling its scent with that of freshly baked bread. He waited his turn patiently in front of the crowded counter, watching the courtesy of the shop girl, listening to her and the customers' continuous chatter. At last the girl turned to him with the amused attentiveness of French women and the innocent and provocative smile of certain French sacred images he seemed to remember.

He left with the croissant in his hand and the drawing book under his arm, in case he wanted to sketch something. He held the walking stick as if it were a toy rather than the necessary instrument it had become. He climbed slowly toward the courthouse, his ears still ringing with the chatter of the *boulangerie*. On the right he left behind him a book shop that he planned to return to later. Now his goal was a different one. He found the way so familiar as to put in doubt the actual passage of time: not even the shops seemed all that different.

A little farther on was the entry to the theater, and from there on the left the three arches of the courthouse were clearly visible. From the open passageway, as if it were a theater set, he caught a glimpse of the southern transept of the cathedral. He stopped, crumpled the paper bag of the croissant, and put it in his pocket.

Nothing in the world would have induced him to throw it to the ground.

THE ATTENTION OF THE QUEEN was now concentrated on the colors. Since her ugly drawing had miraculously overcome the earlier obstacle and the royal project seemed suddenly clear to the artisans, it had become a question of composition and detail, the exact shadings and tonalities of the rich wools through which shadows and highlights had to play.

The queen was impatient to see not the beginning of the work, but the work accomplished, yet had to be content with the labor of imagination in front of the white cloth, which every once in a while she had brought to her workroom. The cloth was carefully unrolled, and as she looked at it, still so intact, the noblewoman imagined the alignment of colors and the unbroken arrangement of figures; and she swung from the thought of the simplicity of the task to discouragement at its vastness. From moment to moment one mood would predominate, just as on a summer day threatening clouds alternate with blazing sunshine. Only the first touch of needle on cloth would still such changeableness. Underneath it all she knew they would be accomplishing something truly extraordinary, and it wasn't so much the skill of the draftsmen or the daily diligence of the servant girls who had woven with her the meters of linen that made her certain of the greatness of the accomplishment: she knew that lay in the skill of the needleworkers.

The women who had responded to the call and come from every corner of France and who now waited patiently for the last royal summons to begin were three hundred. In the village the royal project had been already so fully discussed that the women became aware of the villagers' sense of them as privileged: they were looked upon with admiration and tended with care, as if they were some kind of royal wet nurse breast-feeding the king's firstborn. The few local women skilled at embroidery had become the leaders of a group of sacred dancers, proud of belonging to the queen who had conceived such a project: they welcomed the companions who came from Provence or Brittany as if they were ladies, with the proud and secret language of a confraternity.

The needleworkers waited idly for the draftsmen's task to be completed, although idleness was not perhaps the best term for that murmur of words and movements from one house to another, fed by expectation and complicity. The rolls padded with cotton where the needles rested had been unrolled, at least to take out those used on coarser cloth: the patching and mending of poor country tunics and woolen cloaks was a substitute for the time being for the finer embroidery work. Some women did not disdain to tackle the difficult sewing of certain squirrel-fur slippers appreciated by the ladies of the court. It was to be the last pause before the great effort on the tapestry. As the days lengthened into spring and the time drew nearer there was much talk:

a month had passed since the arrival of the women, but none yet knew when the work would begin.

THE STATUE OF SAINT-HONORÉ was no longer there in its privileged niche in the sun, on the southern portal. It had not been there for a long time, and probably Ruskin himself from his first visits had seen it only in its cold place on the northern portal. This French fickleness had not displeased him in this case: a golden Virgin smiled in the place of the old saint of pastry cooks, a Virgin whom Ruskin had nicknamed immediately Our Lady Soubrette. There wasn't the least irreverence in the nickname; it was rather the tender appellation of intimacy, revealing pleasure in domestic and familial terms. The hip of the statue is slightly tilted: the intention of the sculptor was obviously to balance the weight of the child she carries, but he had unwittingly allowed a certain graceful provocation in the woman's natural pose. She is a young mother who shows off her son, delighted and proud to have borne him. All this suggested a mischievous and exquisitely light eroticism to the English scholar: the Virgin of Amiens was a young mother in the town that was the mother of France, and this fugue of motherhoods touched him.

In fact, coming upon the cathedral from that angle was not the best way to see it, for the great building seemed pressed in by the nearby houses, and the street that led up to it, ending just there at the steps, closed it in with a converging perspective that was distinctly uncomfortable. The gentleman's secretary and photographer was clearly aware of this since, some time before, he had tried to place his tripod at this spot and had ruined a number of plates in a vain attempt at rendering the breathtaking soar of the spire. The results had not been good, for the pressure of the buildings weighed against the gray of the cathedral and dimmed its power: a whole morning of trials had led nowhere. Nonetheless his master kept returning to the cathedral from that angle to look up at the sharp spire silhouetted against the sky above the intersection of the transept.

Standing at the beginning of the street, pensively stroking his beard and absentmindedly removing crumbs from it, Ruskin looked and admired. It was not the easy emotion of age that filled his eyes and made his head shake slightly: certain emotions had always been part of him. In his youth the discovery of any small detail or great sweeping whole had had the same effect on him. And the emotion, rather than fade at a second or third visit, had grown with the anticipation, the joy of remembering and the pleasure of recognition. In all those years he had developed a philosophy for affections and returnings: one could fall instantly in love, but deep love needed time. And for him this was more true for objects and artifacts than for people. That was why he had devised a way to dilute the intensity of his responses on his returns to Amiens: he didn't go immediately to the majestic moldings of the western portals, past which one enters and is in the main nave. Instead he followed a ritual route he had studied on the map of the city. And when he looked upon the sweet, smiling welcome of the golden Virgin he had no doubt that was the way.

SITTING ON A WOODEN BENCH by the central aisle in the great church of Amiens, Anne Elisabeth, a needlewoman, prayed for heaven to watch over her journey. The invocations followed the prescribed order: first she called on the omnipotent God, then Christ, the Virgin, the two saints whose names she bore, and Saint John, the son of Elisabeth. The road did not seem so long or so trying; her town was already in the north, and she had merely to follow the oblique light of the sun to the west. It was a well-frequented shady road, and she would not be lacking water. It was not unusual to meet merchants heading for Brittany along the way, so that even though she would be alone, she would have nothing to fear. But mulling over these considerations hid the real reason she was reluctant to undertake the journey: she would be leaving behind her child, too small to follow her but old enough to be entrusted to her father's mother, who was pleased and proud to take her. Whoever saw her tending the child could not fail to remember the honor accorded to her daughter-in-law, a needlewoman called to a court by a queen.

And her husband . . . he too remained behind, and this was a secret regret that Anne Elisabeth would not admit even to herself. She placed her man in the care of the saints with resignation and particular invocations.

Alone in the vast emptiness of the cathedral she sat on, well after the end of her litanies, burdened by these thoughts more than by the idea of the journey and anticipation of its wearisomeness. At last she rose and walked the length of the church practically to the altar, knelt for one last murmured invocation, and left.

On the first night of the journey, already many miles from home since she was a good walker, she had a troubling dream. She saw her neighbor, a beautiful woman whom Anne Elisabeth looked upon with the suspicion that such obvious beauty always awakens. In the dream she recognized her in the wrinkled, shriveled face of a monkey as white as milk. She was terrified by the skull, on which hair rested as if glued in clumps, like a wig that fitted badly on the forehead and left sinister gaps. A smooth, high forehead contrasted with the wrinkled face.

She broke away from the dream with great difficulty, opening her eyes in a strange room she did not recognize at all, and felt a new uneasiness take hold of her in the pit of her stomach, the repugnant sensation of a nausea that rose in her throat without resolution. She had walked far and would be walking longer the next day, but she refused to yield to sleep again, forcing her lids open whenever they slid shut. She held out until dawn, when she was relieved by the recognition of the different and varying sounds of day even before the first glimmer of light.

Her weariness on the following days gave her sleep without dreams, and only awakening was fraught with bewilderment, followed by the need to sum up the distance covered and to plan the day ahead. Finally, as God willed, the woman of Amiens reached her companions, and the court of the queen was before her like a safe harbor. She was lucky enough not to have to share her bed with any other woman: they gave her a room such as Anne Elisabeth had never had in her life. On the chair she organized her few things and the roll of needles, which she unfolded to check the tips, then rolled up tightly. On the yellow cotton the embroidered letters of her name stood out clearly.

*

GEORGE DID NOT LIKE DEALING with the French; he looked upon them with suspicion, seeing in their courtesy an evident sign of hypocrisy: he would not be lured or enchanted. Merely to make things difficult for the cab driver, when he was seated he gave the name of the hotel in a strong English accent, and when the man did not understand he repeated it with greater impatience, but with no change in intonation. It was a preventive revenge for the inevitable mispronunciation that would hit his ear in a short while, that "Oui, Monsieur Ruskìn, bien sur," with the heavy accent on the second vowel, despite the precise and unambiguous "Sir Ruskin" with which he would introduce himself.

His official duty, once he had deposited the luggage in the room that he would carefully examine, was to order dinner and make sure of a discreet table. Then he could consider himself free for the rest of the afternoon. In fact, within this apparent freedom lay George's real task, a task to which he had had to adapt himself now for some considerable time, and in which he had become extraordinarily skillful. The day before the journey he had been called to a private colloquy with Miss Louise, a distant and not very young cousin of the master, who had been in charge for some time of the peaceful domestic running of his lakeside home.

The nature of the interview was already known

to the valet; it was simply a question of reassuring the lady of his own trustworthiness, about which he had already given ample evidence on other occasions, during a number of journeys to London and Oxford.

In this case the situation was more complex, and his task heavier, but George gave all assurances. He must simply not neglect to take account of a particular characteristic of the master, a characteristic that had been manifesting itself more and more obviously in the last few years and in various circumstances: the gentleman particularly liked to explore the destinations of his journeys in solitude. These journeys had been fewer, and they had led back to places he already knew well, as if he no longer had any wish for the new, but sought comfort in the familiar. But during these visits, sometimes, with no apparent reason, he had suddenly lost the sense of place, had found himself disoriented and baffled and had had to ask for information. Why and how this happened was not clear to anyone, but it happened and the gentleman was the first to be hurt by it, even though he never said anything. George's task involved the whole of his discretion, and the ability to watch from a distance to safeguard his master's desire for solitude. This too was a late eccentricity, after all the years of wanderings in the company of his father and mother. They had been the ones to lead him to the discovery of Europe. Or perhaps they let themselves be led by him, by the fascinations and explorations of this son who seemed their visual mediator. From the first time, when the young John was fourteen and they had set sail from Dover, he had undertaken that journey again and again, always bearing with him something of the family, at the very least the promise of a daily letter for his mother to study and to read anxiously between the lines.

Now it was George's less gratifying task to study anxiously, since that time when, no longer having to account for himself, the scholar had become prey of that subtle sense of loss. A trifling but strange condition, the valet thought, looking out the window of the cab as it started. A few steps away the gentleman was heading toward rue Trois Cailloux, his usual approach to the cathedral. George leaned back in his seat and pulled the curtains across.

WHEN THEY BROUGHT the first sketches to the queen, and they were really as she had imagined them, she studied them for a long time; she visualized them on the cloth and was utterly convinced that the extraordinary achievement was possible, that it was certain. She felt the joyous relief of one who sees an inaccessible way suddenly leveled. The only threat now was the impatience to see the end of the work. As she ran through the story that she and her companions would transcribe onto the cloth, she was fully aware of this danger. But artistry and intelligence would make an ally of the obstacle of time that now frightened her: day after day patient construction would be a substitute for the anxiety, stitch after stitch in the cloth; in the attention to detail the writing would grow naturally and become whole.

She was thinking all this with the drawings in front of her on the table, after dismissing everyone with a peremptory gesture. Stroking her forehead lightly, she tried to estimate how long the work would take. In order to know she had to make comparisons, but where to find embroidery of parallel vastness?

The embroidery on her wedding dress, which had seemed an enormous task, bore no comparison to this, even though they had told her of many hours of skilled labor just to compose the geometric and floral patterns on the skirt and veil. The hours spent on the linen cloth in front of her would become months, perhaps years; the first day would barely be remembered by the time the last one dawned. But the queen was a practical woman: everything begins and ends in time, and time is in God's hands. That thought stilled her. Her task was to organize the labor wisely: the embroidery could be done only in full daylight, and the summer months would be the most profitable. From October on they would have to limit themselves to the midday hours, and days of rain and

snow, when dusk reigns, would slow down the work
and keep the needlewomen idle, waiting patiently for
sunlight, the sunlight that at this moment, in the first
days of June, blazed at its height. The queen saw it
rise, squandering so much of its light, wasting it on
nothing. And the lightness of the first summer eve-
nings filled her with restlessness, because she didn't
have the work in hand and could not yet move her
project on. In the meantime she had prepared the
wool skeins, arranging them by color, and had dis-
tributed the work among the women: in the strategic
arrangements of the embroidering she felt like a master artisan in his shop, distributing the work to his
apprentices. Sometimes she flattered herself a little
with the more masculine comparison of the align-
ments for a battle. The roll of linen, still wrapped
and untouched, waited to be unfolded in front of the
needlewomen, as a battlefield at night waits for the
morning's conflict.

All that was left now before the women could
begin was the tracing of the design onto the linen, a
task of the utmost delicacy, which the most skilled
of the draftsmen had been called on to perform. He
worked in the royal suite for seven days, followed by
the fascinated eyes of the lady who watched the agile
movement of the hand on the cloth, which left behind
it the shape of the drawing, like a map devised so
one would not lose one's way. The queen sat in front

of him, idle and silent, but gaining more deeply in assurance and knowledge of the work to be done.

The draftsman at the end of his task received a golden chalice from her, which was much more valuable than the fee agreed upon. It was given to him by a member of the court before he left the palace.

THE CATHEDRAL of Amiens has, so to speak, the big and rough voice of peasant wealth when it celebrates its ceremonies; the thick-set God of the main portal has the same voice, affecting as He does the sturdy and distinct features of a man of Picardy. He is barely credible as the son of the golden Virgin with the swaying hip and the fine, delicate face.

Ruskin had dedicated himself to her for some time, from his first visits to Amiens, drawing her repeatedly. He had penetrated carefully every feminine feature of the small Picardy Lady, and had finally seen the kinship between her and the man. And in some young woman or girl he came across in the town, he would notice the beginning of that maturity that flowered in the statue. The Virgin seemed younger than her son: in the Annunciation she had the shadow of a pout, and now from her still place in the niche warmed by the sun, she gloried in the past travail, presenting to mankind the fruit of her labor and hope, and imagined her son already a man with his hand raised to bless his Picardy brethren.

The pleasure in the contemplation of the stone world of the cathedral had led Ruskin both in youth and in his full maturity to compose a kind of drama, so that every statue told its story and lived in a dimension incomprehensible to man. He had toyed with this fiction many times, taking up the game from precisely where he had left off the time before, as if he was following a kind of chess game in which the pieces moved on their own and returned to their original places, leaving behind them illegible but clear traces.

Ruskin's eyes were no longer those of his youth. Focusing now was a great effort; the boundaries between each image had become uncertain and had faded in a haze where even the sound of voices was deadened, with that effect by which the shortsighted are also a little deaf. But as one draws near, the mist fades and the outlines become definite, until finally the observer can see still outlines and mocking details that a minute before he had sworn he was not able to grasp and to hold.

Ruskin was very close to the portal of the Virgin now, and she was distinct even to him when he lifted his uncertain eyes to look at her. He was slightly dizzy from the tiring effort to overcome that barrier of mist from which the figure emerged. He smiled, recognizing her. But he was really smiling at her, and would have liked his valet with him at that moment to witness this encounter, someone with whom to speak of the face of the young mother, the friendly head bowed in an ageless pose that defied the passage of time. So many years had passed since his last visit, but the golden Virgin did not seem to resent this; she wooed him still, with the shrewd sweetness of youth.

ANNE ELISABETH had never seen the sea; and the sea was close to the village around the court of the queen. So, on one waiting day, the woman of Amiens walked there. The meeting was subdued: she removed her shoes where the grass gave way to sand because she wanted to touch the water. As she drew closer, she felt the sand grow moist under her feet and she gathered up the hem of her dress. After a few more steps she bent forward, offering her upturned palm in the gesture she had learned was the gesture of friendship toward animals. She waited until a small wave advanced to bathe her feet, rinsed her hands, and passed them over her face and hair. Then she returned to the grass, content with this second baptism she had given herself in the mild seawater.

Every body of water is different. The Somme, with which she had the familiarity that every washerwoman of Amiens had, was severe, icy, and slow in comparison with the constant fluctuations of the sea and the friendly traces it left on the beach and the soft, moist sand. Walking back to the village under a midday sun that warmed her without bearing down heavily on her head, as it did in the summers of Amiens, she thought of the things they said in the village about the queen's tapestry. They said there would be a great expedition on the sea, with the sails of ships spread out over billowing waves. Masters of embroidery know that it is not enough to follow faithfully the drawing traced: the expert needlewoman must be in possession of the nature of the drawing, to give to it with each stitch the appearance of life, sometimes life itself. The vibration of a wave lies not only in the perfect placing of the woolen thread, and the passing of the needle in the cloth follows an interior movement that is not exhausted by the mechanical gesture. It had been necessary for her to look on the sea.

Anne Elisabeth had learned her art as a child (in adulthood it can no longer be learned, not even with the best teachers), and she had exercised it watching herself severely, as if she were observing some other self. She feared no other judge apart from herself, and she handed over completed commissions certain of the praise and the admiration. Only those who did not understand failed to be in awe before so much perfection. Anne Elisabeth was not arrogant, simply conscious of her talent.

The queen too knew how to embroider: her training and her work was no less than that of the woman of Amiens. She had the nimble hand and the sharp eye that did not fill with tears even after hours of work on linen. Like the woman of Amiens, she was ready to measure her skill against the talent of the three hundred women she had called from every corner of France.

THE GOLDEN VIRGIN showed an essential and attractive youth, all the more attractive for Ruskin, in whose mind the idea of motherhood had left a dark shadow that had accompanied him from the most distant infancy, and had receded only in his mother's last days. He had not assisted her except for brief periods when his cousin Louise rested in the next room. Of those moments by his mother's bedside he remembered the smell of medicines, which he had never been able to stand, the shallow breaths, and the half-open mouth. He gazed at her in troubled bafflement: the last witness of his first world, the ancient terrestrial paradise of childhood, so full of prohibitions, so crowded with precepts, was abandoning him, leaving him bereft and a hostage to memory. He himself was no longer young, and after his mother he supposed that there would be no one left who would precede him in that last journey, that he alone would be the one to follow her. But this melancholy consideration was not enough to erase an opposite sensation of light and lightness, the circle of shadows receding to show the transparency of a sun from which they had kept him, as if from some kind of corrosive energy.

Not even the solemnity of death prevented him from considering how, in fact, he had never loved his parents, with whom he had simply lived the instinctive exchange between animals. They had protected him, and he had filled their time with preoccupations over a child whose nature was too gentle, and an adolescent who was still too pliant. But in the years of his young manhood the trust between him and his parents had been damaged, and he carried with him the unpleasant sensation of bearing something broken that he did not have the courage to throw away, a little like a cracked tooth whose sharp edges are smoothed by the constant movement of tongue and saliva.

He had been away from home when his mother died, just a few steps away in another neighborhood, looking for a doctor who might be able to lighten her last moments of tribulation; he did not ask himself whether it was fate or determined awareness that led him away just at those moments, although he had certainly mistaken a street that he knew very well, and by that mistake he had wasted precious time. But he remembered also that he felt not the slightest anxiety when he found himself on the other side of the district. Mrs. Ruskin opened her indefatigable eyes on the void, and the niece sitting by her found difficulty in closing the inquisitive eyes that still seemed to watch.

The eleven-o'clock sun hit the spire and slid along the side of the cathedral until it touched the top of the portal where the Virgin bore on her outturned hip the weight of the child, proud of that burden. From up close, it seemed as if the child squirmed in her arms, following some kind of ideal trajectory of escape. But it was an optical illusion: the stone mother and child were destined never to be separated.

DRUMS ANNOUNCED the royal edict: the following day the queen would welcome the three hundred needlewomen in the hall of the palace and the work would begin.

A great room had been chosen high up in the castle where there was no barrier against the sunlight at any time of the day. They said—but perhaps these were snatches of the rumors that fed the curiosity of the villagers—they said that the room had not seemed big enough to the queen and that a wall had been knocked down. Three hundred seats placed in a large oval around the circumference of the room were the only furnishing: from the narrow windows the sky dominated everything, and on the northwestern side the shimmering sea was visible in the distance. Each hour of the day gave its particular light to the room, up to the sunsets that blazed on the plain. In this way night time seemed slow to arrive.

The evening of the vigil, with no ceremony, the queen had taken her own seat to the tower and placed it on the western side, in the part of the room where the oval narrowed. She was the only one to accompany the servant who bore the bench and to watch him place it among the others. She then dismissed him; she would come down alone after closing the door with the keys she would be carrying on her for a long time to come. In the deep silence she prayed in a clear voice for a successful outcome to the task to which she had consecrated herself. Meanwhile the luminous, still summer night had fallen, slowly the contours of the room faded, and the towers outside and the distant sea disappeared.

The queen would have liked a sign of consent from above. She waited, but no sign came and she left to return to her well-lit suite of rooms in some disquiet; but why should there be any sign after all? The miracle would be happening through her own will and hand, and the hands and will of the three hundred needlewomen.

Standing by the window of a small room in a house built into the walls of the castle precinct, Anne Elisabeth thought of the house in Amiens where her daughter perhaps no longer asked after her, since a child's memory is puny and the distance between them boundless for the child. The needlewoman had an impulse of jealousy, because the memory of man is also puny, and only beasts never forget. She stretched her fingers and made them dance: the black hair that teased her husband's thoughts and passed by him invitingly every day would lose its sheen long before Anne Elisabeth's hands had aged and could no longer hold a needle.

Laid on the altar in Amiens on the most solemn feast days was a white cloth: white embroidery stood out on white, the sign of unparalleled skill. The name and craftsmanship of Elisabeth were embroidered in the curl of the acanthus and the plumes of the bird of paradise, forever.

AS MIDDAY WAS APPROACHING and it was not a feast day, there were not many people around the cathedral. Perhaps that was why the regular tap of the walking stick on the cobbles seemed the only sound as the gentleman crossed the street. Hearing the sound, Ruskin remembered the time he had stood with his father in the main nave and heard a continuous whir of wings, implacable in the silence, until they had caught sight of a swallow destined to die in a frantic and exhausting search for air and a way out, high up on the cross beams under the roof. He had felt sorry he could do nothing to help the bird, but remembering this, he thought that he would feel less compassion now, knowing it is a common fate to die exhausted after a vain search.

It had happened to him, for example, to whom they had given the prophetic name of John. Every name, whether one likes it or not, is a kind of blueprint of the destiny of the bearer. And he had obeyed, he had cried in the desert—a crowded room is no less a desert than the arid sands of the New Testament—just like the saint whose name he shared and whose relic, a fraction of the head brought from the Holy Land, was kept in Amiens. Who knows whether his love for the Picardy cathedral sprang from this, like an ancient and involuntary affinity that lay buried in the deep well of memory, beyond what his mother's positive Christianity had taught him. In fact, Mrs. Ruskin had neither appreciated nor liked these stories of Catholic miracles, these moral inheritances that were so distant: they had called him John because that was his father's name and, if there was an inheritance, it was the clearly visible one of his father's family history.

However, his mother had thought of the future

of her gifted child in very clear terms, to separate him from the world of trade in which he had been raised; with this aim she had used circumspect strategies, of which he was completely unaware, taken up as he was by the passions of a solitary boy. His very absentmindedness had been disarming and had dismantled or at least deflected the maternal intent, as any obstacle deflects the trajectory of a bullet. Mrs. Ruskin believed in all sincerity to be preparing him to be a preacher, a stern bishop with keen eyes and a persuasive tongue. Her idea was not born of nothing, because the young Ruskin did not lack the requisite characteristics for this vocation, or at least the outward traits, accompanied by a passion worthy of great causes. And Mrs. Ruskin felt that religion was a great enough cause.

The obstacle that deflected that almost perfect plan was unexpected, and had seemed something completely harmless. But it was to be, that before which the mother's stubbornness would be obliged to yield. The whole family lingered in front of a birthday present, imagining travels and peaceful adventures. Ruskin was never to forget with what benevolent defiance to the habits of the household they began to contemplate for the first time the thought of a grand tour of Europe—the timorous anxiety with which he watched his mother's waverings, her nays and yeas, the youthful enthusiasm of his father, and finally the countdown to departure. Because they finally did leave. The gift, the precious present, had been Rogers's *Journey to Italy*, with illustrations by Turner. Its influence was not exhausted in those first months, and the book became rather the way by which the boy discovered his real vocation, and was to defeat completely Mrs. Ruskin's strategic skill. The fourteen-year-old boy found something that entered his blood and never left him.

As for Mrs. Ruskin, there was nothing for her to do but raise her eyebrows, swallow her disappointment, and try to see the side that was not yet spoiled: art could be a form of praise to God.

FAITHFUL TO THE PLACE and the hour, before the sun had risen, the queen and the three hundred needlewomen were up. Three hundred women had waited patiently for that day, and finally they left the houses where they were guests; well in time they took to the empty streets, barely lit by the first light. In certain alleys the walls of the houses were so close to one another that they seemed unwilling to let the night escape into the air, cobbles and beaten earth dragging down the dark of the shadowy sky.

In the silence of her room, the queen, like a skilled watchman, heard the rhythms of the different steps coming toward her. She dressed, took up her cotton roll with its needles, unrolled it, and counted the needles one by one, testing the shining points, then rolled it up again and went quickly down the steps to the entrance hall. She was impatient to be joined by her companions, impatient to see them, with the restlessness of those who want to avoid all preliminaries and begin.

When the rattling of the gates resounded in the courtyard, she herself opened the heavy portals of the palace, without help from the servants. But at the echoing of all those feminine voices coming toward her, she took a step back and felt faint: how could she ever have thought to control and command that number of women and to lead them to completion. And suddenly the specter of chaos flashed before her, the infernal chaos of a work done arrogantly.

On the other hand, her appearance silenced the voices and the needlewomen stood poised and breathless, waiting for the commands of the queen whom none of them had seen or heard before. In the expectant silence of the hallway, the queen knelt, and immediately there was the flurry of the women who followed her, the rustle of skirts; a new silence followed this momentary confusion, and finally the royal needlewoman intoned a psalm from the morning Lauds, in a dry, distant voice to which the hesitant and improvised chorus of needleworkers responded.

Anne Elisabeth had glimpsed above the heads of her companions only the black of the royal dress; she would have wanted to see the face of the queen, but she was not quick enough in rising after the amen, and her companions again hid the queen from view. It was day when they began to climb the steps to reach the tower, and then again the woman of Amiens glimpsed a flash of black dress, the dark veil, and the high sash around the chest—more like a nun than a royal wife, she thought—and then she too caught her breath in surprise at the enormous room and the ordered alignment of the three hundred seats where most of the women had already found a place; only a few were still empty. At the opposite end, where the oval narrowed, she saw the queen's bench, even though nothing distinguished it. Next to it, on the right, there was one empty seat, and the woman from Amiens took it. The murmur around her had grown again, heartened by mutual curiosity and reassured by shared confidences in half whispers.

The queen had passed behind Anne Elisabeth while she was busy looking at the hall, and Anne Elisabeth found her suddenly seated by her. Nothing of the figure could be distinguished under the wide dress; the face was white as milk, the forehead high and smooth, with the hairline invisible behind the black veil. The eyes too were black, black restless eyes that moved around the room. Strange eyes, shadowless, as if they had no lashes.

IN A PAGE of *The Bible of Amiens*, Ruskin makes a curious observation: "The outside of a French cathedral . . . is always to be thought of as the wrong side of the stuff, in which you find how the threads go that produce the inside or the right-side pattern." To how many other historians and scholars would this parallel spring to mind, with its strange domestic comparison, born from familiarity with a house and the haberdasher's? What comes to mind is the expert hands of a merchant stroking the back of a tweed, along which also the observant eyes of a woman run. In the case of Ruskin it was a question of method and experience, a way of observing that had its own raison d'être. The existence of the extraordinarily big runs parallel to the existence of the extraordinarily small; from two opposing poles radiate paths that by the most immense routes eventually meet, and from a certain distance from this point of convergence X, a cathedral and a carpet reveal the same nature in their elaboration, an identical network of bearings, slender threads and heavy pillars stretched to sustain bold vaults. As a child Ruskin had often tried to penetrate the arabesques of a carpet, concentrating before the labyrinth of colors, which he tried to de-

cipher with an effort and patience that forced a frown
on his forehead. It was a strange passion for a child,
but the room in which he spent so much time was
bare of games and toys, and his activities had to narrow down—or expand, it depends on the view-
point—to what nature and the space inside and out
of the house provided. In the long term Mrs. Ruskin's
choice was educationally correct: "He must not get
used to any superfluities." This was the unopposed
sentence and he, the object of this sentence, never
thought to rebel against it. So to his eyes the carpet
in the drawing room, to which every other child
would have been indifferent, took on an incalculable
value: he imagined the skilled hands of a distant
carpet maker as they tied thousands of knots to make
the pattern, so swiftly that the eye lost the sequence.
The house in Herne Hill had many, variously shaped
carpets, and each combination of color, pattern, and
geometry seemed enchanting to the child. In his
imagination each weaver worked on one carpet,
tended it, and constructed it day after day to say what
he wanted to say—even more, to make it speak its
own language of color and figure. And so the child
gave himself to deciphering those formulas of writing,
the secret language of the carpet, as if he were a
cryptographer. From the outside nothing was visible
except a certain aptitude to stare absentmindedly,
which his parents thought was the result of his sol-

itariness; his mother tried to redress this by imposing on the boy long sessions of reading and transcribing Bible passages. And so in the mind of the child, weavers and prophets moved in overlapping spheres and constructed kindred languages of mysteries and prophecy.

As for architecture, he arrived at it much later, but dedicated himself to it with as much devotion until he discovered where the labor of his ancient imaginary weavers and the words of prophets could meet without any strain, in the stone that does not hide its external sutures, while within, in the hollow of the temple, it is one continuous tapestry.

IT HAD BEEN like shifting a heavy cart stuck for a long time, dragging and pushing it until the level ground tilted into a slope, and from there accompanying it so that it would not pick up too much speed and crash. The red signs left by the draftsman flashed along the whole length of the cloth and seemed live in the hands of the women while they fixed the edges of the linen to the frames.

The queen's ambition was that her tapestry speak to the common people and to the educated. The cloth therefore told in images a complex story of wars, while on its upper edge the needlewomen would be following with their embroidery the obscure outlines of a language unknown to them, a message in which they took no part.

The needles had been threaded in various colors, and finally the work began: it was still only a preparation for the embroidery itself, a kind of basting, over which the full embroidery stitch would be added. But the first stitches were enough to relax the tension, and already some of the women, finding themselves instantly at home in their skill, were singing to themselves as they worked. They had to work as if they were a single pair of hands and this involved an identical slackness—no nervous gesture to tighten the woolen thread; but consciousness and pride in their skill freed the fingers, and the work was taken up in perfect orchestration. From the very first day they worked intently, exploiting to the last the light of the sun they saw rise on the horizon, stand poised during the middle hours, and then glide toward the sea.

Sitting next to the royal needlewoman, Anne Elisabeth kept her eyes fixed on the cloth: she was disappointed not to be working on the waves, which she saw were in the hands of the queen. Tight-lipped, silent, she worked, adding stitch to stitch with a swift, careful hand; with no indecision she covered the red outline precisely. After a while she sat back to look at the first basting. The figure sketched only in outline was that of a horseman and his steed moving in a light trot.

Anne Elisabeth's royal companion was slower, but the care with which her arm accompanied the needles and pulled at the thread showed her skill; absolutely confident, she did not pause to look on the work accomplished. In any case, she was not curious, for the drawing was familiar; her anxieties lay elsewhere, in the risks of teamwork and the harmony among the women she had finally put to work. At this thought she had a sense of vertigo, as if she were a guide who had led a group in a nighttime expedition through the narrow gorges of a dangerous valley.

Her shoulders, bent to so many hours of work, were beginning to burn and trouble the woman from Amiens, who lifted her head with a sudden movement; the facing windows were flooded with the full midday light. The queen's head was bowed, proceeding in her work unrelentingly.

THERE WAS A BEGGAR by the main door of the cathedral of Amiens; he's still there, and whoever happens to visit the church will come across this indistinct figure, curled up without showing his face. It's not easy to give him an age, and one can barely guess the sex. Ruskin had met him on his first visit to the cathedral when he was merely a boy who accompanied his parents on the grand tour. They had been the ones to put in his hands the coins to give the beggar, without arrogance, with the courteous gesture of the gentleman. Some years passed before his next visit, but the young gentleman was recognizable in the gesture of giving to the beggar, who, like the other of long ago (if it was another), kept his lids lowered and his hand stretched out. Ruskin saw him again each time he returned to Picardy; we too can see him, the beggar who is as immutable as the stones of the cathedral and will remain as long as the church dominates Amiens.

Seeing this perseverance, Ruskin asked himself of what was time made, along what tracks it ran for each man and woman. The time of the beggar and of the golden Virgin seemed the same, slow, almost imperceptible to human measurements. How lonely did the gray-haired gentleman feel, whose eyes were only slightly dimmed, how much closer to the end than they; it seemed to him that no one immediately after him stretched out a hand to take up what he would leave behind. Time consumes itself indifferently in seconds and millennia; the proportion varies only in its nuances, just as solitude can be experienced among a hundred absentminded people or with a single listener who questions with an insistence dictated by affection. But the hour is more destructive than the millennia, the bereavement over one, more painful than over a crowd that fades, indifferent, into the past; at least, this was what the gentleman thought he had learned in all those years.

When Ruskin, from the other side of the street, caught sight of the beggar against the entrance, he searched his pockets. He had never had any doubts as to the appropriateness of giving him money, as if it were not for him to judge. But he hated the movement of looking for coins, lingering in front of the stretched hand to pick the least valuable pieces. Then he crossed the street, bent with some difficulty over the man crouched in a niche of the doorway, and placed the coins in his hands, careful not to let them clink. The man seemed asleep and perhaps did not notice the gesture. In any case he did not thank him.

THE PLACE THAT EACH WOMAN had occupied on the first day became her permanent place, and Anne Elisabeth from then on was the queen's companion —she alone, because on the other side sat an old lady-in-waiting who did nothing except observe with curiosity the work of the needleworkers. When the old woman didn't come, no one took her place.

The woman from Amiens had found her working rhythm and was embroidering fast; without even realizing it, she was measuring herself against the queen, in an unspoken race. And the royal woman

was steadier and more constant than even Anne Elisabeth, never lifting her eyes from the cloth or her
hands from the needle. Just a few days had been
enough to dim the emotion of the royal proximity in
Anne Elisabeth's mind: she had soon become used to
the black nun's garb, the milk-like skin that seemed
never to have seen the sun; but the habit of proximity
was indeed strange, and its strangeness returned to
her at night, as if that particular figure had lodged
itself in one part of Anne Elisabeth's mind. In the
moments before falling asleep, the figure of the queen
dissolved in the air of the room, but left the sign of
her presence, like a distinct obstruction. So the mind
of the needlewoman was not free, and in her sleep
she had to contend with small but irritating difficul-
ties, narrow passages that shortened her breath with
anxiety. And often she preferred, as she had the first
night after she had set out, to remain awake. With
her eyes open in the dark, to which she would slowly
become accustomed, she questioned her anxiety and
unease, but could find no reason. She knew well how
in a fever these meaningless anxieties came to the
surface, and even though it had never happened to
her, she remembered distinctly the agitation and wild
words of a companion of hers in Amiens, when they
were still girls and she had fallen victim to an in-
curable illness.

But Anne Elisabeth's body was healthy; the hunger that woke her at dawn and the pleasure with which she ate said enough about her strength and how nature followed its course without hindrance. During the day the effort of the work, which grew in proportion to the growth of the achieved embroidery and to the miracle of whose development at the hands of so many she was witness, absorbed her completely and she forgot the nightly unease, the memory of Amiens, of her child, of her husband. So it seemed to her, but the discomfort of the nights never left her until morning, when the fragment of a presence dissolved in the sun.

In the tower, as the mid-afternoon sun inclined toward sunset, the women worked to the accompaniment of dim exchanges of confidences and the old lady-in-waiting badly drawling a lullaby. It was very hot and the light was intense. With a sudden and swift movement the queen undid her veil. Pressed to the nape of her neck, punished for its abundance, the hair fell onto her shoulders like a black, shining wave: the oval of her face was still framed by the black band around her temples, and the splendor of her head of hair came nowhere near the paleness of her face, suddenly free and bare. The features of a woman were suddenly revealed to the needlewoman from Amiens, and the nunlike severity put to flight. The queen was beautiful, with the beauty of the head-strong and willful. Anne Elisabeth was right to fear her in the secrecy of her soul.

EVEN THOUGH he had seen grander things, Ilaria del Carretto had been and remained the most seductive woman of his life, the most fascinating encounter, because the sculptor had fixed the features a second after death, when all travail was forgotten. In looking at her it was difficult not to believe in the momentary repose of a quiet sleep. Ilaria could be found within the very consciousness of peace, in the certainty of those lids closed against the anxiety of light: there was no message of rest more reassuring—sent down the centuries to each visitor who paused by her or bent to study her face—than her whole body composed for eternity. Having always had by his side restless and uneasy women and men, and being himself unstable, Ruskin remembered looking at her with envy, and then feeling a surge of tenderness for the composure of the young woman at whose feet lay her dog, asleep—as if she had wanted to take with her on her journey only the docility of the little animal.

In his young manhood Ruskin did not have many feminine role models, perhaps none other than his mother, whose granite firmness was closer to the foreboding of an impending storm than to the serenity

of settled weather. As for the young women he had
occasionally met, and for whom in his own way he
had even fallen, none had made him pause for any
length of time in that idea of peace that seemed to
him at times to be his greatest ambition in the middle
of the contrasts that he experienced hour after hour,
day after day, without any possibility of a solution.
That Ilaria's serenity was the serenity of death did
not scandalize him or worry him. He remembered
instead, in an intense flash, his father's disquiet. He
had been as charmed as John himself by the face of
the woman from Lucca, to the point of forgetting
that it was marble, and that the material was perhaps
the reason for such beauty. While the son had seated
himself in a patch of light, to draw the features and
the soft folds of the clothes, his father sat next to him
in the shadow and could not take his eyes away from
the marble bed on which the young woman lay.

They stayed long because the subject of the
drawing was surprisingly complex, never adequate or
faithful enough to the model; every once in a while
they were disturbed by an occasional visitor who did
not have their persistence and left quickly. When they
returned to the square they were bothered by the full
light and a certain embarrassment in resuming the
conversation. They walked through the narrow
streets looking for a café, and reached a tavern set in
the walls of the town, which gave onto the little square

of San Frediano, where children they found singularly unattractive were playing, with a disturbing clamor.

"Think what order, what discipline," his father said suddenly, "to go like that, without perturbing anything around, without confusion. It would be a great thing. But one cannot know, one cannot predict." His son looked at him, surprised at the sudden preoccupation that he had never heard him voice before. Now the older Ruskin was betraying a painful restlessness. "Of course not," John said finally, almost irritated; but to himself he qualified it, convinced that one died as one lived, and therefore there was nothing arbitrary or uncertain, no need to question oneself if one already knew oneself well.

They returned to Pisa too late, and the cab driver swore frequently along the way because of the darkness. The old gentleman seemed to have buried the impressions and melancholies of the afternoon that he had unintentionally shared with his son. He had reverted to daily living. On the Lungarno, a little before the hotel, the cab passed close to Santa Maria della Spina, the church that seems lapped by the river. The young Ruskin, still in the grip of his father's painful words, looked at the church as if it might bring him both comfort and unease. His father's mundane, inappropriate words came back to him: "What shall we give the cabby, John? It's our fault we're so late." His angry whiplash of an answer remained with him for a long time.

His father died some months later, discreetly and without confusion, just as he had lived.

ON THE SEVENTH DAY, as God willed, the queen established a day of rest for the needlewomen, and she rested herself. That morning the door of the tower was not opened, and the room remained silent. The cloth lay like a giant, seeming to rest from the continuous needling of the embroidering, and the much worse stretching by the vise on the frame which had been loosened the night before to allow the linen to recover its original shape, distorted by the passing back and forth of the thread.

One of the orders of the queen on the first day had been that the needlewomen should always have clean hands, and she had had put next to each bench a rough towel with which they could wipe their sweat during the day when the work and heat weighed on them, and so the cloth was spotless—not a shadow marred its cleanness.

On the seventh day the queen went to the tower alone and let herself into the room. "Where are you going, your majesty, on the day of rest, when you know it is sin to work?" the old lady-in-waiting had complained, but the queen had not answered and had wanted no witnesses or companions. Indifferent, she went past the searching glances and took the steps to the tower slowly, looking out of the arrow slits at the view that changed on each turning of the steep staircase, becoming vaster, more distant, as far as the sea that glittered on the horizon.

When she reached the room, she examined the embroidery sections one by one, sitting at the seat of each needlewoman. The work was just sketched, and in some cases the small needlepoint hardly impinged on the basting. She tested them all to see the compactness and lightness: it was a test of skill to maintain the pliability of the linen, as if the embroidery were adding no weight, with no intertwining between the threads and the weave of the fabric. It required a particular sensibility to the texture of the material, both a delicacy and firmness of touch, like that of a mason who barely nips with his chisel to fashion a low relief, as if it were a natural part of the stone he has in his hands.

The workers whom the queen had called to the court were accompanied by a reputation for extraordinary skill; but no mother really believes in the reputation of a wet nurse to whom she must entrust her baby. The queen read carefully the embroidered history, tested it to feel the thickness of the figures like a blind man who recognizes features with his fingers.

The three hundred women had worked in perfect harmony as if by a single hand, and the eyes of the queen filled with light at the sight of such perfectly orchestrated skill. She then looked at her own part and examined it with the same critical eye. She did not suffer from any conceit, but neither was she needlessly modest, knowing full well that she was one of the best needlewomen in France. She studied her work with the same severity with which she had looked at that of the others, and with all the detachment of which she was capable. She found she was no less skilled than many of her companions, no less skilled even than the excellent needlewoman on her right. Even more importantly, she found that she could not distinguish her work from that of the three hundred women. She found that this evenness, in which every hand seemed to become absorbed in the whole, was what pleased her most. Pride is multifaceted and is no less in those who hide their name and conceal it within the magnificence of a project and its realization, choosing to be submerged by it. Such was the pride of the queen.

AT THE CENTER of the nave, seated on the bench where he himself used to pause in his previous visits to the cathedral, Ruskin noticed a young woman— a local woman, he thought. She seemed to be waiting for someone, and meanwhile she looked around without much curiosity, to while away the time. Seated as she was, with such great simplicity, she reminded the old gentleman of the time when a cathedral was a public place, open to dispute and conversation. He sat too, carelessly letting his walking stick drop to the ground. He was not that old, but his bulk somehow justified the awkwardness of the gesture. The woman, who turned with mild curiosity at the noise, made no gesture to rise and pick up the stick lying crossways and abandoned on the ground.

The interplay and meshing of spires and the heavy fretwork of the front disappeared on the inside, with the pure outline of the naves. There was nothing of the ornate majesty of an oak forest or the particular exaggeration of northern woods. What reigned was order, the severe pace of the light around which the columns formed geometric shapes.

For a long time during his life, Ruskin had not in fact understood the idea of order, which he had associated with the squalid and the haughty. But it was the tidiness of rooms that irritated him, the rigid straight lines of Italian gardens that seemed to smother any freedom: as for himself, he had deepened only the knowledge of God's discipline, in which he had to walk as he had been taught to do. But he walked within it with all imperfection: this is a sign of honesty in man, when he tends toward that which he will never achieve in this life.

The light of the last window dimmed gradually along the sides of the column and fell in a last reflection on the shining floor. "To what point my spirit has been paralyzed by the errors and griefs of life, to what point my knowledge of life has been inadequate. What could it have been if I had walked more faithfully in the light . . ." This thought was suspended, unanswered and most probably unanswerable.

The woman in front of him had meanwhile risen without hurry and with no signs of reverence for the holy place; she turned and began to walk toward the doors. She moved with a slight sway of the hips, stopped undecided in front of the abandoned walking stick on the floor, bent and picked it up. On his part the gentleman watched her with no gesture of thankfulness when she leaned the stick against the bench, and followed her with his eyes as she continued with the same unconcern. She was a young woman, younger than her statuesque body would lead one to believe, and his gaze followed her for as long as his shortsighted eyes allowed him to see her. From the inscrutable end of the church he heard the heavy clanging of the door as it closed.

*

IN THE GLIMMER of first dawn, Anne Elisabeth lingered in bed and watched the rising of the sun. She had woken early as usual, but this time she looked around and waited before getting up. With her eyes open and with her mind ready to make contact with the day, she remembered that this was the day of rest and that for the first time in her life she had a day for which she did not have to account to anyone. It was also true that since that pervasive unease had shortened her nights and stolen from her sleep, waking up had been difficult. But she owed to her wakefulness a small discovery that was in its way reassuring: she had a roommate, a mouse. It was absolutely normal to find mice in houses, especially those near the city walls and close to the countryside, and Anne Elisabeth was neither frightened nor disgusted by these little creatures. This one was small and pointed, and the first time that the woman had seen him, was intent on a singular exercise. Before catching sight of it, she heard an insistent rustling and a minute thud every so often. She searched the corner from where the noise came and saw this tiny gray creature trying to introduce itself in a hole high up in the wall. In a vain attempt it jumped on its hind legs and projected its clumsy body toward a safety that was completely out of reach; each time it fell on its tail and each time it returned to its original position and with immense efforts it tried again. It was ridiculous to watch it, but the woman's amusement was soon tinged with pity; it would have been enough for her to stretch out her hand to take the creature to the hole, and she would have done it too, but as she was about to stretch her hand the mouse suddenly stopped dead in its tracks, and kept as still as a salamander in the grass, waiting for the danger to pass. Now both were stock-still, two enemies paralyzed by each other's presence, asking themselves who would make the first move. Anne Elisabeth sat up in bed of a sudden, and the enchantment broke in the mad race of the mouse toward an invisible hole.

The needlewoman let an instant pass, looking around and making no noise, then rose and dressed, taking care to shake her apron free of the few crumbs that were still clinging to it. Every morning from then on, she would take care of her little prisoner, of whom she never again found any sign except in the consistent disappearance of the bread crumbs.

It was the morning of the day of rest and she had woken early. She gave long, careful time to washing herself, and to cleaning and tidying the room, as she would never have been able to do in Amiens, where she had to tend her child, her husband, and the whole household; when she was working, there was no difference on feast days. But today was a feast day indeed, with the voices of her companions walking by the house on their way to the fields. She could follow them, there was nothing to stop her, and she did indeed follow them for a while, asking them where they were going. But they were an aimless and confused group, and Anne Elisabeth soon left them, suddenly thinking to go in the opposite direction, to walk through the village and take the road to the castle. Perhaps it was habit, or a listlessness when confronted with a new way, she didn't know. Certainly she let the chattering group of women go and remained on the verge of the path before turning back and going past the doors of the village. She remembered the hard voice of the queen when she had dismissed them the night before: "Loosen the cloth from the stretcher and tomorrow give yourselves a rest. Rest your shoulders and your eyes for the work ahead." She had a sharp note to her voice, like a thorn.

Anne Elisabeth passed in front of the portal to the castle, left it behind her, and turned right, taking the way to the sea.

RUSKIN STARED at the walking stick in front of him, in the empty church: the young woman of Amiens had an ease in her movements, a royal bearing, as if she had been educated in some kind of court to be a lady. The scholar's imagination—as some called it with admiration, and others with irony—followed the delicate hips of the girl from there, from the church bench, as if they were those of a dancer. He had chanced to see, a long time before, a feminine figure of the same fullness: she sat on a throne, distant and absentminded, languishing in a kind of boredom and melancholy that no initiative or action could change. The body was hidden by heavy clothes and was without age, but the face was young; if only she had risen, at the first step all that lassitude would have dissolved from her features, to linger perhaps in the downward slant of the sulky lips. And the serried dancing of the walk would have acquired the grace of contrasting movements.

The figure that stood before him in his imagination, evoked by the woman from Amiens, was Italian: one of those irresolute beauties by Botticelli whom he thought he did not like because they were attenuated, and yet so attractive! He saw himself as he had been ten years before, with the straight, martial stance that indulged neither his own weaknesses nor those of others; virtuous and scornful he walked the dirty streets of Florence searching for a long-lost world. He remembered to have removed from his thought as if it were temptation that relaxing of the face and figure in which the Tuscan painter was such a master. But now all that repugnance touched him less and he enjoyed the young woman of Amiens; she didn't have the joyous and flirting energy of the golden Virgin, she was not a mother, and yet he was attracted by an exquisite enchantment.

He would have gladly followed her without asking himself where. Certainly with her the fragment of a new world would be revealed to him: and the first mystery would be her name, and with the name her voice. For a while now he had found himself curious about voices, like someone who has emerged from a world of silence and recognizes the worth of sound. He didn't remember seeking out voices so much before, he had not even yearned for music. . . .

The woman could be unreachable now; or she could be in the square, still waiting with the same distant unconcern. The gentleman rose, and picked up the walking stick energetically and without leaning on it, in fact holding it skillfully under his arm, as he moved toward the entrance at the end of the nave. He opened the internal door, then the smaller external door, and he was in the crystal light of late afternoon. The square was empty.

ON THE EIGHTH DAY the work drew back to the tower the three hundred women: chatter about the Sunday filled the room with excited voices, some weary from lack of sleep. Anne Elisabeth had nothing to tell her neighbor who was quizzing her on her absence from the village feast, which most, if not all, had attended. And she told the woman from Amiens how she had danced and danced well into the night and how she had eaten in wonderful company and . . . she was taken up completely with the memory of the good-looking peasant who had, with smiles and gestures, taken her home because of course she could not go alone. Anne Elisabeth's neighbor was not at all attractive; the low forehead and the expressionless eyes were not lit even by the pleasure of the previous night.

The queen was the last one to come in, with her head bowed and hidden by a long veil; behind her pranced the old lady-in-waiting. Silence spread in the room. The cloth still lay abandoned: it seemed enormous and live with the flashing of the red design already pursued by the variety of colors where the embroidery was full and finished.

Before beginning the work the queen admonished them from her seat without raising her voice and without inflection. It was a voice that neither frightened nor comforted, but was strict and commanding. She wanted what had been done up till now to be a sign of total dedication without pause. Some of the women thought that she was reproaching them for the rest she herself had ordered, but it was not so, for she then allowed cautious praise of what had been achieved: the effort of each one had given the hoped-for result, but this was the mere beginning;

the labor of the future could jeopardize the present, their hands could still fail. It was strange how the voice of the queen could remain low and still be heard perfectly by all, even when it became quieter yet in one final bidding: "Our tapestry is a votive offering that will be received in church. I want it to be no less than the work of master stonemasons on a cathedral, I want it to be equally powerful."

Anne Elisabeth had kept her eyes lowered, glancing at the section of cloth on her lap, but she knew she was being watched intently by the queen with a look that was of defiance. Immediately afterward the cloth was stretched again, the vise tightened around it while expert hands smoothed out the smaller creases. The section to be embroidered was perfectly straight and taut, and the great machine of hands began again, in a continuous and varied staccato.

Anne Elisabeth had threaded her needle with blue and began her day.

THE FIRST PART of George's task was concluded with no complications: the room they showed him for the master was fine, and his own, just next door, lacked nothing. The suitcases had been placed with care, and those things that the gentleman treasured particularly, especially the daguerreotype plates, had been put away where they would not be disturbed.

Seated in an armchair in his room, George allowed himself the luxury of a long cigar. His name was not George, an annoying detail since names have their weight in the life of an individual. His name was John; he had the misfortune to be called by the same name as the master he had been serving and following for so many years, an unfortunate homonym that Mrs. Ruskin had unhesitatingly abolished not to create confusion: she had decided the new baptism in her authoritative way, magnanimously granting him the choice of the name. From the depth of his heart George had not forgiven her this insult; he had been slow in assimilating the resentment, and even years after the death of Mrs. Ruskin it emerged at times, turned against the son, whom he nonetheless served devotedly, to whom he was bound by trust, respect, and the habits of a long acquaintance. Unlike many others close to the gentleman, he had been able to see clearly the particular though not always perceptible characteristic of the scholar, the refuge his mind took in the labyrinth of infancy and the losing of himself there as if in a city forgotten for years, of which one may remember the streets but not where they lead to. The specific form of this obstinacy in returning was worrying, because no rational consideration could drag him into the present, no evidence: one could only wait until this quiet crisis had run its course, until it stopped with the same arbitrariness with which it had started. What was needed was patience and coolness, that was all.

Time to enjoy the cigar, then he would go downstairs to wait in the lobby for the master's return: really he should not leave him to wander in Amiens on his own. But George knew perfectly well where Ruskin had been heading, and had been further reassured in the morning: rue Trois Cailloux, the cathedral that he would not fail to visit as if it were the first time, then a walk around the exterior to look at the soaring arches, and he would return to the hotel. It was all predictable, there was no reason why he should follow him. Tomorrow he would have to be available all day for the photographs the gentleman would ask him to take: this was something he would have enjoyed doing much more if they did not limit themselves so strictly to stones, those residues of time, and never photographed, for example, a woman. Not even Miss Gray, in the brief spell when she had been Ruskin's wife, was honored by a photograph. He whiled away the time smoking until it was five o'clock, then made his way downstairs to arrange for tea.

*

THE NEEDLE THREADED in blue was for the remnant of sea that faded into the white of the sand where the ships would berth. Anne Elisabeth, in her section of cloth, picked up the last edge of water on which the queen played her embroidery of ships that plow full sail on the sea. That was why she had not been attracted to the feast and the courting by a handsome Norman: the woman from Amiens liked dancing and being wooed, but something the previous day had instead driven her toward the sea. She had gone there alone and without encouragement had taken the little-frequented path to the dunes; and she had had time to think and imagine herself submerged and enveloped by water, as she had never felt any desire to be imagined before, because the Somme was muddy and the ponds around Amiens frightened her.

She had slid from the high dunes with her heels planted in the sand and then had run gracelessly, tripping at every step until she reached the wet boundary between earth and sea. Looking down at her feet she saw herself mirrored in the thin sheet of water above the sand that altered constantly as the waves changed, in a continuous movement. She ventured farther than she had done the first time, with hesitant steps, gathering her skirts in a clumsy bundle, catching her breath at the iciness of the water against her knees and the spray soaking her dress. Holding the skirt was useless, and she let it drop so that it billowed out all around her before becoming laden and dark with water. The water was up to her hips and she was not sure whether to laugh with pleasure or cry out in terror. She turned back toward the shore, pursued by the sea, which dragged at her; not knowing the language of the sea, she did not know whether she was being lured or threatened.

On her way back at the height of the day, the hot air dried the dress on the surface but left on her a subtle dampness that refreshed her legs. At home she took off her petticoat and hung it on the chair, looking at the small patch of dampness drying on the floor: during the night, the little mouse would have to go around the wet patch in its search for food.

The last stitches of blue were finished, and the needlewoman threaded her needle with the green and then the dark brown of the legs of the boys who, bare to the thighs and with no shoes, were dragging to land the ware from the ships. With great skill she suggested the imperceptible pressure of the low water against the shins and the knees of the carriers; the queen, glancing at her neighbor's section of tapestry, perhaps recognized the effort toward truth that was engaging the woman. Then she returned to her own work.

*

GIRLS ON THE THRESHOLD of adolescence and mountains seem to have in common the perception of their
inviolability by those who approach or seek them out.
It is true that step by step they erode this inviolability,
but these steps are never enough to annul it. The
young woman of Amiens had vanished, swallowed
up by some obscure corner of the ugly city that protected her.

Ruskin went down the few stairs and turned
back to look up at the cathedral lit by the lusterless
sunset: it seemed massive and tall, like a mountain
peak. Ever since the remote nature and lure of peaks
and high clouds had seduced him, he had contemplated mountains, and among the eternal breath of
their universality and inaccessibility, had understood
the distance between desire for possession and the
capacity to attain it. It is the same inviolability that
the best mountain climber thinks he is conquering
when he plants a flag to designate the place of his
passage, without realizing how useless the act is, just
as the greed of those who stake out a piece of land
and claim it as theirs is useless.

And so Ruskin's mature and then senile attrac-
tions were toward certain creatures whose features
were still undefined, like a sketchy outline that time
was preparing to chisel more certainly. What could
be born of the imprecise line of an adolescent chin,
of an androgynous chest on which even the most

studied clothes fell like heavy blankets? When he saw in mothers some trait of the girl, perhaps a pout of the lip or a certain slant in the glance that was a sign of the future of the adolescent, he was filled with the melancholy and pain of his decline, and his imagination pursued the wrinkling of a marble forehead and the curling up of hands whose fingers, filled with rings, simply underlined their age.

The only thing he could do for himself was to maintain inviolate the secret attraction of this inviolable age, and let it be companion to his pursuit of what man can do when he aspires to imitate God. He, who had caressed with tenderness the marble face of the woman of Lucca, would never have laid a finger on the cheeks of one of these child-women.

As the sunset faded, the outlines of the cathedral became absorbed in a heavy blackness at once clumsy and threatening. It was the real face of Amiens. From the other side of the square, crossed occasionally by a carriage, Ruskin could no longer see the portals, a piece of the rose window, or the projecting lateral turrets. Only a few carriages and no one on foot: life was continuing in another part of the city, far from the cathedral, which was left like a float abandoned off shore. It really was time to go back.

*

THE QUIET WASH of sea by the berthing of the ships was no longer enough for Anne Elisabeth, and on the second day of the second week she advanced her request: "I pray you, Lady, to entrust me with the embroidery of the sea." The woman from Amiens was standing in front of the queen's seat. Her companions thought that the emotion of such audacity had made her forget to bow in supplication. But she was not a suppliant: she asked with such firmness as to be equal to the queen, who had lifted her head in amazement at the worker from Amiens, and met level and unflinching eyes.

During those first days of work rumor had spread about the severity of the queen: the veiled and austere woman, so like a nun who has forgotten her age, would be a tyrant on occasions; anyone who made a mistake even on a single stitch or who crumpled the cloth had better beware. The women awaited with apprehension the breaking out of a storm. The red outline of waves on the open sea had barely been basted on the queen's frame: Anne Elisabeth was asking to take the queen's place, and she was asking with a tone of authority.

The storm did not break and the terrible nun-queen felt no resentment: the morning air poured in from the windows, so charged with energy and light, that it seemed like the sign for which the queen had prayed ten days before, of a blessing on the work about to begin. Only the old lady-in-waiting started when she saw her mistress rise and entrust the woman from Amiens with her frame; she started without quite knowing what had happened and not daring to ask. The woman from Amiens's pulse did not miss a beat and her hands gave no tremor when she stretched them to the cloth and touched the red outline. As a child she had gone to launder clothes at the river and she remembered the roll of the grass on the banks as it followed the current of the water; her fingers followed the weave in the same way, with the same docility. She worked skillfully around a portion of cloth and hid its harshness under the woolen thread. Then she went back and fashioned the keel of the boat cleaving the waves; she worked on the shape of the ship, the layers of wood grooved one within the other so perfectly not one drop of water would pass through, not even in the worst storm.

ON THE LEFT SIDE of the cathedral square and not too far from it, ran the river that branched out in the many canals that had given Amiens the name Queen of the Waters a long time before. This name, which Ruskin had immediately noted, was by that time completely inappropriate: the river was slow and muddy, the canals had little water, and a great stretch of imagination was needed to see any majesty in the squalor of the dirty banks where sheep and horses pastured. But what the present no longer gave was still abundant in the memories and fantasies used to reconstruct the past. Why not imagine an age of splendor and clean industry under the crust of black soot that now darkened the houses and the streets? Amiens had been a capital, wealth had spread far and wide, in the merchant homes and the palaces, through the labor of men and women, in a land of wise industriousness. Amiens had been "skilled like an Egyptian in the weaving of fine linen; dainty as the maids of Judah in diverse colours of needlework. . . ." In this way Ruskin liked to think of it, setting the imagination of the past against the present.

As he contemplated the bulk of the cathedral, it had seemed natural to him that there should have been a time of wealth, but not in an age of gold that tempts to evil riches, but in an age of cloth, of looms, of weaving, of embroidery, a patriarchal and domestic season. A season of women, and finally of one woman—like his adolescence, the experience of which he had magnified to contain the world. As he stood in the darkening silent square and followed the contours of the river under the hill, he had no difficulty in seeing a mosaic of busy, boisterous figures. Behind them, still undefined, the geometry of the cathedral, the imposing outward walls culminating in the large wooden beams of the vault, under which would be preserved the precious relic of the fragment of the head of John the Baptist. It was a purely imaginary world, to which Amiens had probably never corresponded, just as the world of Dante's Florence or of dogal Venice, which Ruskin idolized, had also probably never existed. Or any other place in a time of good government: if such a government has ever existed.

Once the sun had set, the damp cold began to penetrate through to the bones. The gentleman would have done well to hail a cab and ask to be taken . . . but where? Not yet to the hotel, nor in pursuit of the figure vanished who knows where, who may have been watching him from one of the windows that gave on to the square. Without thinking of a goal, he walked slowly down to the road that flanked the Somme.

THE DAY HAD PASSED and the queen, alone in her room after nightfall, was incapable of sleeping. Very strange, as it was strange that she had been unable to touch food at supper and had followed the conversation so distractedly that silence had fallen quickly. The old lady-in-waiting would have wanted to ask, but she did not even dare to formulate the question. She thought that the boldness of the embroideress that morning had something to do with the Lady's mood, but could not bring herself to mention it.

After reciting the prayer of Compline with the lady-in-waiting, the queen retired, leaving the old woman to wonder; but when she lay on the bed, she could find no way of going to sleep. It was a night lit by a bright, full moon, and from the window of the royal bedroom the town was more clearly visible than during the day: she could see the roofs of the low houses, the higher bastions of the walls, the black of the countryside beyond, and on the horizon she could picture the invisible sea.

She returned to bed and left the shutters open, looking up at a patch of sky: she could not see the moon, but she knew its presence by the large band of white lighting up the sky. But she could not sleep even like this: the white light induced in her a rest-lessness, a fever that made it seem a sin to be resting, having embarked on such a great task; if she could have done it, she would have called all the courtiers, because surely no one, like her, could think to sleep under so much light.

A little later the queen was climbing the stairs to the tower. She had conquered the uncertainty of the corridors in the semi-darkness without a torch, letting her eyes get used to the black of the walls and the floors, until she had reached the workroom. The light from the arrow slits lit the steps, and she could clearly see every one and move securely. At the top she felt the handle, opened the door, and stood, letting the size of the room, the three hundred empty seats, the long white cloth, take shape around her.

In one of the last houses at the end of the village, meanwhile, Anne Elisabeth was resting in perfect sleep.

AT THE HOTEL, where George had been waiting a good half hour, tea time had passed and there was no sign of the gentleman. The valet, or secretary if that was what he was, was in default because his place was in the street, secretly following his master, not sitting in an armchair, even if he was on the edge of it with anxiety. On the other hand, Amiens was a small town, and for the gentleman it was concentrated at the cathedral, so it would have been enough to head toward the square through the cluster of old streets. George would undoubtedly find him around there, intent in reading one by one the writing on each stone of the church: there was no doubt about the meticulous obstinacy he had always shown in these things.

But with all this, the master was not returning, and the late dusk no longer allowed explorations of the mysteries of sculpture. George was nervously smoking a cigar that deserved more attention to its fragrance, and bent his head to look toward the door every time the opening and closing of it made him hope. Two gentlemen speaking with a strong Welsh accent came in, and discussed at length the advantages of a room in which they would be staying only a couple of nights. George remembered the gentleman's descriptions of his youthful travels together with his mother and father, an extremely patient and gentle cousin, and a kind of footman or lackey who did everything. Their arrival, Ruskin had told him, was always a source of momentary disorder and bustling, watched over by the suspicious and expectant mother and counterbalanced by the father's wish to smooth things over and minimize any possible differences, for which the older Ruskin was immediately sorry.

What emerged was a tableaux halfway between the merry and the fussy; Ruskin still remembered these things with an intensity that placed them outside time, and could recall the smallest detail, the half words and the inflections, as if it had all happened the day before. It was strange, this aptitude in him to erase the obstacle of the years, and not be able to remember what happened half an hour before; it was strange and moving. His schooldays, his infancy, twenty years had no depth; like the work of these Italian primitives, they were like a long sequence of parallel strips that ran along inside him and were never exhausted and never joined up completely. Mr.

Ruskin never seemed to have lived in time, George thought, or at least time had enveloped him but never touched him: he was the child on the beach in Cornwall who gazed curiously at the waves reproducing themselves constantly, he was the Oxford student, the adolescent in love with Turner and useless spouse to Miss Gray, or again the easy traveler completely bound to an impenetrably solid family structure, or . . . Without wanting to, even George entered into this game of recollections that his master had confided to him with the sober fluency of the great narrator. From a nearby bell tower he heard the hour strike: it was six. He stirred, noticing that the Welsh couple was no longer in the lobby, and outside it was night. He took his coat and walked out.

THE EYES CAN easily adapt to night and conquer the first aversion to the dark that seems to deform contours: the white of the cloth stood out in the room, and soon the outline of the embroidery began also to emerge clearly enough to be seen. The colors could not be distinguished, but the darker and lighter tones stood out against the white. The queen walked confidently to her seat and took the section of cloth on which the young woman of Amiens had worked, embroidering the sea; like a blind person who touches to recognize, she felt the fullness of the embroidery, followed its roll, felt the line of the waves lapping the flanks of the ships. The woman of Amiens had used all her skill, and her art had responded fully. It was a perfectly tuned instrument.

The queen rummaged in the pockets of her dress and found the roll of needles, and maneuvered as best she could in the darkness, looking for the wool to thread. It was no longer night, the dark was merely a friendly shield for her project. She threaded the needle in front of the window, in the clear, milky light of the moon, made a knot at the end, and put the first stitch through from the underside next to the last stitch made by the woman of Amiens that evening. She was working in senseless conditions—embroidery needs full light, certainly not the shadowy light of the moon—but she could not sleep, gnawed by an unease that had robbed her of sleep. On one of the ships, one of the larger ones that Anne Elisabeth had taken from her, the rudder was unfinished: the woman of Amiens had sketched out the light outline but left the middle empty. It was a small patch, difficult to embroider even in broad daylight, but the queen was possessed by a defiance and not even the absurdity of this night work seemed such to her. Stitch after stitch she executed the work, and the ducal vessel raised the cross of its main mast, received its rudder. What in the daylight would have taken less than an hour took such a long time and was such an effort that the otherwise perfect hand of the royal needle-woman made the mistake of covering the wave with the embroidery of the rudder. She realized this only when the eastern window lit up with the first light of day and the shadowy shapes took on form and color. The ship was complete, and, bearing the sign of an imperfection, it plowed through the sea majestically. The queen had in her mouth the bitter taste of a sleepless night, an uncomfortable heaviness, and a confused perception of being unable to find rest. She left the high room and took refuge in her bedroom, where she lay on the bed. Three loud knocks on the door and the cutting voice of her lady-in-waiting called her to wakefulness after an incalculable time.

GEORGE LEFT THE HOTEL when night had fallen, and started on the trail of his master. He followed the spire of the cathedral, which he glimpsed from the streets, like Ariadne's thread and reached the southern portal, the one where there was the statue of the Virgin that the master never tired of praising. He went the whole length of the narrow street that led to the portal, and saw a beggar still by the doorway, hoping for some late coin. But his head was bowed forward, as if he were sleeping, and the stretched hand seemed abandoned. George ignored him, looked in from the door, and peered down the dark, deserted nave. From there he could see nothing and, despite the reluctance to enter the damp cold of the interior, he penetrated farther, along the whole central aisle, searching the darkness of the lateral chapels, stopping near the empty confessionals. He sought at least a clue to the passage of his master, a glove forgotten on a bench, a pencil that had slipped from a pocket. But he found nothing. And yet he had been there, he had left some imperceptible sign of his presence, something like a chair shifted from one place to another in a room.

When he reached the end of the nave, he forgot the respectful action of turning back to the altar— his master had taught him that, believer or nonbeliever, the turning back to the altar before leaving was the sign of consideration toward a home—and pushed against the velvet curtains to return to the square quickly. It was dark and the river below was barely visible. Laden with mud and darkness, the water of the Somme crawled toward the bend that wound it around the hill; the hill itself was indistinct. George's search had ceased to be logical; the pressure of time accompanied and disorganized him, and he now moved following simply a sensation, a simple instinct. He went toward the river, sensing on his right the bulwark of the cathedral, and he imagined it like some mythical creature coming down to the river from the mountains. No one came to the banks of the river at that time of the evening.

His master meanwhile had attained his goal, following the wave of memory, and had reached the summit of the hill on the other side of the river. Night made the work of memory that much harder; the sign of the streets and the clues noted some time before had faded. But if he had forgotten the streets, his father's steps were still clear, and the bridge over the Somme toward which they were walking. They had been tired after a long day, but had not wanted to forfeit their evening walk. The full atmosphere of what had seemed then an insignificant evening came back to him: they had been accomplices in escaping tea with his mother and cousin Jean, and breathed deeply the damp evening air that his mother claimed was so bad for him. He remembered that in his enthusiasm and impatience he had strode ahead of his father, and then waited for him at the top of the slope. He had tasted again just then, after so long, the saltiness of blood in his mouth, the sign of the old weakness, and had been irritated by it. Being alone for a few seconds more had allowed him to wipe any trace of the insidious disease, hiding then the badly folded handkerchief in his pocket. When his father had reached him, they had turned to look down at the dark, indistinct form of the cathedral: he was certain at that moment that his father was sharing his own emotion, and was proud to be bearing it for him.

"It looks like a mountain," his father said simply, and the young son by his side smiled at the poverty of the comparison. Now, years later, he was still in front of that jewel of Amiens and it was indeed a mountain: where God had not wanted to designate the imposing structure of mountains, and had accumulated stone on stone to witness his desire to exalt himself. As old now as his father had been then, he read the signs in the way that once he had amiably derided.

The walking stick kept step with the slow, heavy, obdurate pace despite the slope. As a child he had asked for the story of Babel and the confusion of language to be read and explained to him, and then had asked himself how was it that God had not confounded the language of the builders of Canterbury Cathedral. And looking at the cathedral of Amiens, the sculptures, the saints in their niches, the healthy peasant face of God or the motherhood of the golden Virgin, imagining the stonemasons and carpenters at their task in a time of hardship, he thought he understood the heavenly indulgence.

At the top of the hill a few houses flanked the road and then left it. In a second, he lost all memory of his thoughts, and, turning in astonishment toward the road he had walked, asked himself where he had come and why. George would look at him with disapproval for being so late for tea.

"Your mother will not fail to grace us with her sulks. . . ." The old gentleman and his son had turned back almost at a run.

THE GREEN, transparent waves lapped the thighs of the servants as they carried off the ship the merchandise and the food stores needed by an army on foreign soil. They were small crystal waves, so close to the dunes it was easy to guess the sandy bottom and the precarious balance of the men.

The representation was as faithful if not more faithful than a painting: Anne Elisabeth was running through the cloth backward, but stopped in astonishment at the rudder of the ducal ship. She remembered leaving that section of embroidery unfinished the evening before because it required particular attention and the light was fading. How could it be that someone had stolen into the room, which she had been the last to leave, and had stolen also the pleasure in work that cost her such effort and feeling?

Anne Elisabeth was sitting on the left of the queen's old lady-in-waiting, who had just come into the room, alone. She had given no reason for the absence of the royal needleworker. The woman from

Amiens was a positive woman, but for a second she doubted reality, doubted herself and did not dare take up the needle, could not feel the serenity that had accompanied her work up till then. The other women had also observed the empty place, but they had almost disregarded it; in fact, they felt freedom from the sense of constraint that the queen's presence cast on them and they felt lighter. The old, nagging lady-in-waiting was nothing in comparison to the young queen.

Anne Elisabeth took the cloth in hand, shifted the fixed margin to the top, and tightened the vise around the bottom edge. She threaded the smallest needles with the dark green and brown of the lower arabesques. Two birds of prey were poised menacingly with outstretched wings and open beaks, ready to attack each other: the draftsman had firmly outlined the barely contained aggression of the two animals, and the movement of the woman from Amiens took on some of the same quality of the gaping beaks and spread wings as she covered the red line. When she took her hand away from the embroidery, she paused a moment on the rudder, above the band of the edge, and looked resentfully at the interrupted line of the waves.

All day there was no news of the queen in the high workroom.

*

THE REVELATION of old age had come to him in Venice. When he was still young he had walked the city, venturing down even the most sordid passages. He had paused at the corner of the ducal palace, of the Ca' d'Oro, of the Ca' Giustinian to transcribe the beauty of the stones, and through the daily labor of close observation he had discovered the degradation of the sculptured figures, the erosion of limbs and joints as if they were human, made of bone and flesh. The morning dampness in the alleyways and the small squares and the vapors that rose from the canals were seductive but corrosive: below the beauty of the architecture that faded into water he imagined the slow wear of the foundations on which the lagoon had been beating for hundreds of years. In fact, everything that surrounds us beats against us and corrodes us from the first day, from the first moment of our existence, but for the twenty-year-old Ruskin the discovery of the world of art and the possibility of transcribing it in his drawings had made the long journey of decadence by Venice fascinating. The water of Venice, the persevering accomplice to time in the quiet canals and the deep lagoon on which the buildings were reflected in permanent transience, did not intimidate him as much as the northern coast on whose beaches he had spent time as a child, burdened with maternal cautions against the sea and all its dangers—attractive dangers, the snares of which he must all the more carefully guard himself against, watching the waves beat on the shore with their eternal rhythm but without touching them, without letting himself be touched: he would have recognized himself, his real nature in the hurling of the tides, in the foaming of those angry monsters. But he had been educated too well in avoiding them.

The sly peace of the Venetian canals and the peacefulness of the stretch of water to Torcello, with its water barely distinguishable from the sky, like the tired pulse of an old body, turned out to be no less seductive. In his youth he had thought of it as a sign of the varied energy of nature, and had considered himself as one cylinder of this power. Years later, however, he noticed the strangeness of recognizing, in the slower, heavier beat of his pulse the rhythm of the lagoon. And his dedication to rescuing for the future what had not yet been eroded or had died seemed all the more painful and difficult.

He went down the hill to the bank of the Somme, and imagined there too, as he had for the Venice of the doges, the energy of a time in which the city had been a skilled builder—when instead of the foggy skies and the muddy river, a strong, undefiled power struggled to grow. He looked toward the dark mass of the Somme: he had walked too long, all day, and his legs were stiff; he was proceeding with increased difficulty. He wanted to go on, to go somewhere against the current, but instead he had to lean, and sit on the low wall at the side of the street, because the blood in his veins was as clouded as the waters of the river.

CLAPS BY THE DRY HANDS of the old lady-in-waiting marked the end of the work and of an endless afternoon for the women, who had been waiting anxiously for the signal. They had watched her drift into sleep and forget them until late sunset. It had been the silence that finally woke her, the suspended silence of three hundred working women who had watched her and waited anxiously to be sent away, finally free for that day.

Outside the palace the evening was lit by a moon faintly covered by thin clouds. Anne Elisabeth let the crowd swarm and heard the hum of the women grow faint and fade. The workroom was empty, and the steps of the queen approaching echoed and reverberated against Anne Elisabeth's fast-beating heart: she had had no doubt that her unease of the day would lead to something. She saw the queen come in, recognized her by the black dress, because she did not dare lift her eyes to the face. She followed the dress as it moved from frame to frame, looking at each one. The woman from Amiens wondered whether she had been seen, and thought that perhaps she could disappear and postpone a confrontation. But she would not be able to sleep. In any case, the queen moved without haste and examined the work carefully. Alone in the room she had no grandeur, she was no taller than Anne Elisabeth, she was not even beautiful with those eyes without lashes, the face so pale, the smooth marble forehead. Her hair was hidden, punished for its abundance. The woman from Amiens had not moved from her seat; from there she could see the moonlight fade and reappear as the clouds moved past. Darkness had moved too swiftly into the room, though, and it was difficult to see.

Still the queen continued her inspection, like some night creature, without effort, without haste. Finally she lifted her eyes to the woman from Amiens, and they shone in the half light like the pupils of the nightly visitor to Anne Elisabeth's room, the mouse.

MR. RUSKIN and his valet would have had great difficulty in meeting that evening. Up to a certain point and a certain moment, and from an ideal point of view, their paths could have seemed to converge: the gentleman had come down the hill, and George, walking along the side of the river, between the cathedral and the Somme, was actually moving toward him. In fact, George walked confidently, led by an instinct and by knowledge that his master had let him have about him and his mind. He was an eccentric man, but faithful to those things that are normally considered futile and unimportant—as, for example, a street, a house that he particularly liked, some shard of a view, all that common sense would have deemed unworthy of a man's fidelity.

But things didn't happen in the ideal way, strangely they didn't. Perhaps because of some noise, the movement of some creature down by the river, on the water, the master stirred, rose from the low wall on which he was resting, completely lost and with his heart in his mouth. The feeling was unjustified, the darkness barely denser than a moment before, but the sound of the river and the silence of the cluster of houses nearby was exactly the same. "George," he called in a whisper that sounded like a stone thrown into water. He could see the road in front of him, and his shortsightedness broke up the shape of things—a bush could be the rounded outline of a woman; he was uneasy at being so unprotected and remembered that a few steps back a slope led into the town through a continuous meander of houses. Contrary to his habits, he left the river and took that way.

George, who was coming from the other direction, didn't have time to see or recognize the shadow against a thicker darkness. The moonlight was uncertain and did not encourage whoever might be along the bank. And the mass of the hill, looming just behind, was, well, a little intimidating. He stopped, took out of his pocket a cigar, lit it, played a little with the part he had cut off, and started walking again. He was thinking of the surrounding silence, which seemed hostile to him, perhaps only because of his own diffidence toward the Picardy town. The canals in Venice gave the sense of a different mystery, but they were sweeter, more like accomplices, like the Arno in Pisa at the point of Santa Maria della Spina, which he had learned about under the guidance of his singular master and teacher. He moved faster now and felt a blind fury rise up within him at the vain search: he was never going to find him. He had the sensation that he had cried out in an empty room: twenty more steps and he would turn back, he was not going to go any farther than that bush with the form of a woman. From the bell tower of Saint-Leu a little ahead, he heard the striking of the hour. Eight o'clock.

"WHICH CITY do you come from, from which people?" Anne Elisabeth felt the terror of an ambush at the unexpected voice of the queen, and thought she dredged the name of Amiens from her very depths. The queen asked nothing more, and continued the journey from one frame to another as if she were alone. Anne Elisabeth rose from her seat and drew near the window, looking for the companionship of fresh air. She could hear behind her the rustle of the skirts, one step after another as she was coming near her frame; she thought of the mistake of the rudder, for which she was not to blame, and felt only annoyance.

"You are skillful. Who taught you embroidery, woman of Amiens?" Again out of the very depth of her terror she dragged out the words.

"An old embroideress, she was a woman from . . . no, I don't remember where she came from, she was not from Amiens. She was mute, and to teach me she could only show me without words how she worked; I would observe and copy her. She worked slowly to give me the time to imitate her. The mute shout, indeed they do, and she would shout when I made a mistake or when my embroidery did not seem perfect to her. She would shout in one way or another, without being able to say a word. I learned from her, and she was perfect."

"I was taught by my mother; the very first thing I remember is my mother and her ladies-in-waiting around the embroidery frames."

Anne Elisabeth did not dare look toward the queen and did not know what to add to break the silence. And yet she had a precise question, about that rudder that covered the wave, there on the tip of her tongue. All her courage had to come to her aid now, to know who might have a hand so like her own. In the meantime the rustle of the dress was still and no sound inside or outside broke the silence between the two women.

"My mother was a great needleworker." The voice of the queen rose unexpectedly in the dark, like a ringing of a crystal. "She had a perfect hand and intuition for colors. She worked alone on the nuptial blanket, and when I brought it to court, no one could say to have seen anything so beautiful." She's talking to herself, Anne Elisabeth thought, she has completely forgotten my existence. The door was at the other end of the room, but she imagined nonetheless that she might be unseen and able to escape; she felt so unreal in the eyes and mind of the royal woman.

"And yet she never dared to imagine a project of these dimensions. She lacked the audacity to expose herself to the eyes of the world, the boldness of a man when he builds palaces and towers or when he ventures into the confrontation of war." The figure was outlined, stooped over one of the frames, darker against the darkness of the room.

"Are you listening, woman from Amiens?" She had not forgotten her; in fact, she was speaking to her as if she might understand. Anne Elisabeth nodded, a childish gesture of the head in so much darkness: but the sparkle in the queen's eyes showed that the movement had not escaped her.

"And your old mute teacher had no idea she was raising you to such work." The voice had become merry, finally light, so much so that the woman from Amiens dared to move from the window and come closer to her companion. She did it without constraint, freed from a weight: she no longer had any questions; everything was as clear as the clear light of day.

"My hand, woman from Amiens, is identical to yours." The queen stroked the black rudder of the ducal ship with satisfaction. "We were born for the same art and to the same passion." She raised her eyes to meet those of the embroideress.

Probably in the castle, along the corridors and the courtyards there was the movement of the changing of the guards, the bustle and calls of soldiers doing their rounds; but in the tower the silence was absolute.

EVERY CATHEDRAL has its labyrinth. Sometimes it is drawn into the geometrical patterns of the floor and the marble inlays, or it is roughly carved in the stone that thousands of people have trod, eroding the surface and rubbing away any trace of the Minotaur's prison. At Chartres it seems the childish drawing of four-petaled marguerites, around which leaves have coiled protectively, creating a simple path in which it would seem impossible to get lost.

They say that the labyrinth is a symbol of the union between pagan and Christian eras, between going astray and finding salvation: Ariadne held the thread of hope at the entrance of the palace of Minos, to which Theseus tied himself before venturing into the mortal battle. And so his victory had been complete.

The Virgin to whom the cathedrals are dedicated is the new Ariadne, who holds in her hand the skein, the way through the labyrinth of the world. She, no less than the princess of Crete, knows the distraction of man, the fragility of human memory; and they say that not once has she let go of the skein, not once.

The labyrinth at Amiens is as elegant as a chessboard, shining. It looks like a courtly game, and the lady who holds the thread, the lead, glittering with gold in the midday sun, is a shrewd chatelaine used to the praise of her troubadours.

These were strange considerations indeed for a solid Anglican who now, by reason of who knows what impulse, was finding himself alone, completely alone, in the cathedral, whose northern portal had by some chance been left open. He had in fact pushed the door without thinking, expecting it to be as usual firmly shut, and instead it had opened to him, uncovering the silence and the dark broken by the light of candles. In the day, the light from the rose window falls without interruption on the chessboard floor and follows the trail of the labyrinth.

What the labyrinth alone means needs no artful intuition or wisdom of interpretation: it is clearly written between the lines of every person's life and counterposes a truth at the base of which is a revelation of light. It is merely a question of faithfulness. The questions that attend the journey are at times unsettling, at times as useless as hypotheses without foundations and far from even the appearance of truth. And in fact infidelity runs along an identical labyrinth and in the end sends back an identical light. But it is a light reflected in a mirror.

In the half light Ruskin had knelt to see better, and he stroked the black-and-white paving and traced the line of the labyrinth to the center with his finger. It was a strange, suspicious activity, but luckily at that hour the churches are not frequented.

A BLINDING SUN had risen on the town while the queen and her needlewomen were already hard at work on the last of the embroidery. From one hand to the next, identical and brilliant, the taut thread ran along the drawing; the recent dye of the wool was like a varnish, and the sun through the windows radiated its light on the whole work. The talk of the women was made lively by the closeness of the end and the excitement of the results: it was like a show or a narrative by troubadours—the king's and his army's adventure ran along like an exalting procession, a parable of mobile, clear figures. The needle-workers upheld and shared the pride of the queen who had measured herself against the art of painters and stonemasons. Anne Elisabeth, who was embroidering the last waves, in which the hoofs of the horses plunged, was dark in the face, sad. During the night she had dreamed of her daughter: she had not had such a disturbing and clear dream since that first night long ago, away from home on her journey. That anguish, which she had thought she could forget, she thought she had in fact forgotten, rose up again with the sadness. She felt as if she had never seen, neither in herself as a child nor in any other child, a despair as great as the one that had been in the dream on the face of her daughter. It was like the look of an animal that has been terrified, if only once. For human beings it is a passing storm that settles and comes to nothing; even a child as it grows tends to push it away, but instinct does not erase it, and, even after a long time, creatures marked by this terror are recognizable.

Anne Elisabeth embroidered the last waves that lapped the shore: the back hoofs of one of the horses skidded on the sandy bed, while the front legs flashed

in the thrust of a gallop; the head was high, the eye
glittered with life. When she got home to Amiens,
she would embroider again, for herself and for her
child, the bay horse, with its mane disheveled, and
the other, the one behind the bay, with its open mouth
cut deeply by the bit, the one the queen had wanted
embroidered in a wool as dark blue as night.

That day too had flown, and the embroidery
was almost finished. Anne Elisabeth thought she
would not even have the time to return to the sea.
Her daughter was peremptorily calling her.

IN AMIENS at nighttime the horizon was not visible:
the houses that closed around the cathedral formed
a compact barrier, and any foreigner who might have
happened to walk there would have found obstacles
everywhere. The ugly Picardy capital shut itself up
into a black mass at night that was hopeless to try to
sift through. George returned cautious and perturbed
to the hotel; he could only hope that he had been
preceded, that he would find the master sitting at the
table, irritated and vexed by his delay, with the blue
eyes taking on a tinge of malice. He walked at a good
pace the street that led to the hotel, and when, as he
turned the corner, he saw the two lamps lit on either
side of the door, he speeded up even more. He stopped

a moment in the doorway to adjust his jacket and to breathe deeply before going in, perhaps to meet his master, but if not, for some news after all that seeking—anything, he prayed God, any news.

"Monsieur Ruskìn vous attend à la table," the hotel porter warned him politely. The empty dining room embarrassed George completely; it was late, too late for an Englishman: he looked through the glass door and saw him seated, a little stern-looking but not, it seemed, annoyed. He appeared to be looking with interest at the darkness of the street beyond the window, but he had no plate in front of him; obviously he was waiting for his valet.

"Sir, I'm unforgivably late, please accept my apologies." Strangely, Ruskin smiled peacefully and pointed to the other chair.

"Sit down, George, we are both hungry. You look as if you have been walking for hours, at least as long as I have and these few French"—he smiled again and lowered his voice conspiratorially—"could decide not to feed us."

"Yes, sir, thank you. I'll be glad to, glad to eat. Walking is not after all an activity that I enjoy, it tires me excessively, but with the chance to visit Amiens . . . Did you have a good day?" Without waiting for an answer, as if to assuage his guilt, he began to pile question on question—was the room all right, did he find it comfortable, or did he want to change? He would do it immediately, even before eating.

"Of course the room is fine, I don't expect much from hotels. But I think I will retire early. No, not to write. Imagine, how strange, after so long I feel like drawing again. Then, tomorrow morning, I will ask you to come, to take some photographs for me, not many, just a few. I really intend to draw. The cathedral has some details that I think are unreachable with a camera, and I'll examine those while you photograph." He paused to order dinner, choosing carefully and addressing his companion with affectionate gentleness. "You can imagine," he continued, "that it will be necessary to work early in the morning or the light will ruin the work, even though it is true that at this season the light is always inadequate; but in any case the morning is better, the details stand out more clearly. But this for tomorrow. I'll knock on your door at eight, does that suit you?" It was strange that the master should wake the valet, but it was the custom with them, who for the rest of the evening spoke only of French cuisine. It wasn't a long evening: Mr. Ruskin rose early from the table, and put out his light early as well. He did no work at all, and what is more, the next morning at eight he did not wake his manservant. It was George who knocked on his door an hour later, and found him with his suitcases

already packed. He made no mention of the daguerreotype. Master and servant left the hotel before ten,
went to the station by cab, and took the ten-thirty
train for Calais. The train connected with a ferry for
England, and they didn't have to wait a minute.

THE GREAT TAPESTRY of the queen and her three
hundred needleworkers was borne in solemn procession to the church in a ceremony of extraordinary
majesty. In the midst of the women the queen,
wrapped in a black dress embroidered with green,
held her hands joined in victorious supplication. The
long cloth was stretched out on the ground along the
whole length of the central nave, and the three
hundred workers guarded it against the brazen curiosity of the people during the bishop's solemn bene-
diction.

Anne Elisabeth stood next to the queen, as she
had done during the days of working, and watched
that the embroidery not be crushed, those precious
waves on which William's royal army was sailing;
she barely heard the humming rise and fall of the
curious crowd, received upon her and her work the
blessing, and then, as the queen moved, shook herself
and realized she had to separate herself from the
tapestry. The queen was leaving the church with her
head held high, and the procession was reforming

spontaneously, with an order miraculous among the throng of people that surrounded the nave. Slowly everyone would leave; the square was already an explosion of laughter and light. The queen had chosen to feast with the three hundred needlewomen, and a banquet had been prepared at the castle.

When the last person left the church, when even the soldiers had left their guard posts, two young deacons closed the large portal. In genuflecting, they looked down toward the altar, and saw, stretched out on the ground, the tapestry that prevailed over the shadows. It was perfect.

"We can imagine falsities, we can compose falsehoods, but only truth can be invented."

—RUSKIN

On the fourteenth of October 1066, William the Conqueror defeated the army of Harold, king of England, at Hastings. William's wife, the duchess of Normandy, Matilda, wished to remember the conquest of the island by the embroidery of a cloth of about seventy meters, on which the events leading up to the expedition and the final triumph of the Norman duke were celebrated. She then had this tapestry placed in the cathedral of Bayeux. Or perhaps it was an English queen, Matilda, wife of Geoffrey Plantagenet, who, a century after the events, decided on this unusual historical document. The origin of the Bayeux tapestry has remained shrouded in uncertainty, but it is in any case one of the most moving examples of the art of the Middle Ages, and perhaps of any age.

John Ruskin, an eclectic and disturbing figure of the Victorian era, a scholar of Gothic art and a profound admirer of the European Middle Ages, went to Amiens in 1879 for research that led to talks and to the publication of a book called The Bible of Amiens. *The trip to Picardy was his last journey to the Continent.*

The episodes and the links in this narrative are born from a purely imaginary elaboration of the two events.

A NOTE ABOUT THE AUTHOR

Marta Morazzoni was born in Milan in 1950
and attended the University of Milan. She lives in
Gallarate, Italy, where she teaches Italian culture.
Girl in a Turban, a quintet of stories,
was published in 1988.
The Invention of Truth is her first novel.

A NOTE ON THE TYPE

This book was set on the Linotype in Granjon, a type
named in compliment to Robert Granjon, a type cutter and
printer active, in Antwerp, Lyons, Rome, and Paris, from
1523 to 1590. Granjon, the boldest and most original
designer of his time, was one of the first to practice the
trade of type founder apart from that of printer.

Linotype Granjon was designed by George W. Jones,
who based his drawings on a face used by Claude
Garamond (c. 1480–1561) in his beautiful French books.
Granjon more closely resembles Garamond's own type than
does any of the various modern faces that bear his name.

Composed by PennSet,
Bloomsburg, Pennsylvania

Printed and bound by Arcata Graphics/Fairfield,
Fairfield, Pennyslvania

Designed by Cassandra J. Pappas